Stan and his Gran

For Lily, with love

ORCHARD BOOKS
96 Leonard Street, London EC2A 4XD
Orchard Books Australia
32/45-51 Huntley Street, Alexandria, NSW 2015
ISBN 1 84362 458 3
First published in Great Britain in 2005
Text and illustrations © Sarah Garland 2005
The right of Sarah Garland to be identified as the author
and illustrator of this work has been asserted by her in
accordance with the Copyright, Designs and Patents Act, 1988.
A CIP catalogue record for this book is available from the British Library.
1 3 5 7 9 10 8 6 4 2
Printed in Singapore

Stan and his Gran

Sarah Garland

ORCHARD BOOKS

"Oh no! Look at the time," said Mum. "Gran will
be here any minute and everything's such a mess!"
"It'll be fine," said Dad. "Give us a kiss, Stan."
"I can't wait to go to Gran's house," said Stan.

"Here she is!"
called Stan.

"Hallo, my darling,"
said Gran.

"Right, we're off to work. Bye everyone!" said Dad.

"Lots of love! See you later!" cried Mum.

"We'll just clear up, and we'll be off too," said Gran.

Then Stan, Gran and baby Annie were ready for the walk to Gran's house. They always went the same way and they always did the same things.

First Stan walked along the wall.
"Do you want a hand?" asked Gran.
"Not today," said Stan, and he balanced all the way on his own.

And, although he was quite scared,
he jumped right over the gap in the
wall and didn't fall off.

"That was pretty good," said Gran.

When they got to the park, Gran hung upside
down by her knees from the high bar.

"Why do you always do that, Gran?" asked Stan.
"It's good for my joints, darling," said Gran.

Now Gran needed Stan to help her get down.

Then Stan needed Gran to help him get down.

"Here's the tree! You can't
catch me!" cried Stan.
And they ran round and
round and round the tree
and round the tree again.

"Croo-croo," called the bird
that lived in the tree.
"Gloo-gloo," said baby Annie.

"Wait for me!" cried Gran, and then they were off on the last dash to Gran's house . . .

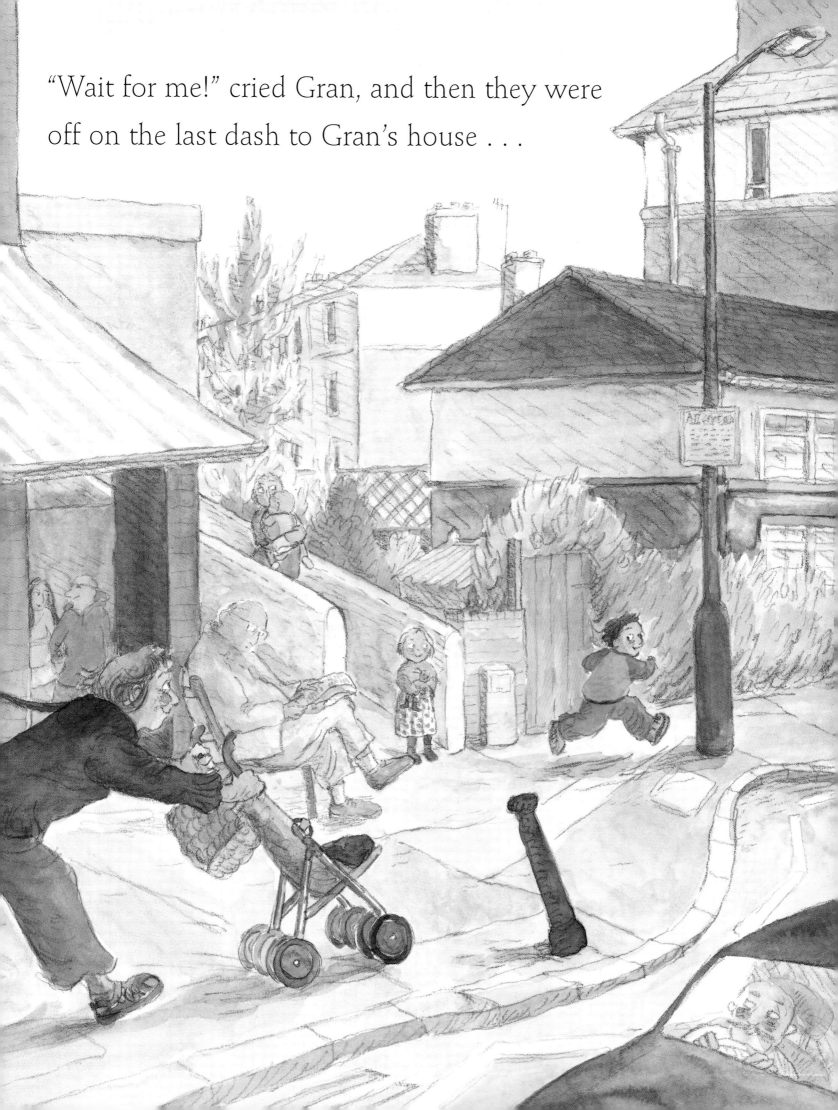

. . . down the street, past the cars, past the shop, past the green gate, all the way to Gran's front door.

Then Gran reached for the key that was always around her neck. And it wasn't there! "Oh, Stan!" said Gran. "I can't believe it! I've lost the key!"

"Lost the key?" said Stan. "But Gran, if the key's gone, how can we get into your house?" "I'm not quite sure," said Gran.

"Is the key in your handbag?" asked Stan, anxiously.

"This bag's full of stuff," said Gran, "but there's no key."

"Mmmm," said baby Annie.

"Maybe it's in Annie's bag?" said Stan.

"Oh dear, oh dear. It isn't here either," said Gran.

"Ummmm-yum," said baby Annie.

Now Stan felt really worried.
He stood and looked at Gran's house.

"What if we can never get inside?" thought Stan.
"Who will feed Gran's cat? Who will wind up the clock?
What will happen to my toys? And what about my lunch?"

Stan sat down on the doorstep
and thought and thought.
He tried hard not to cry.

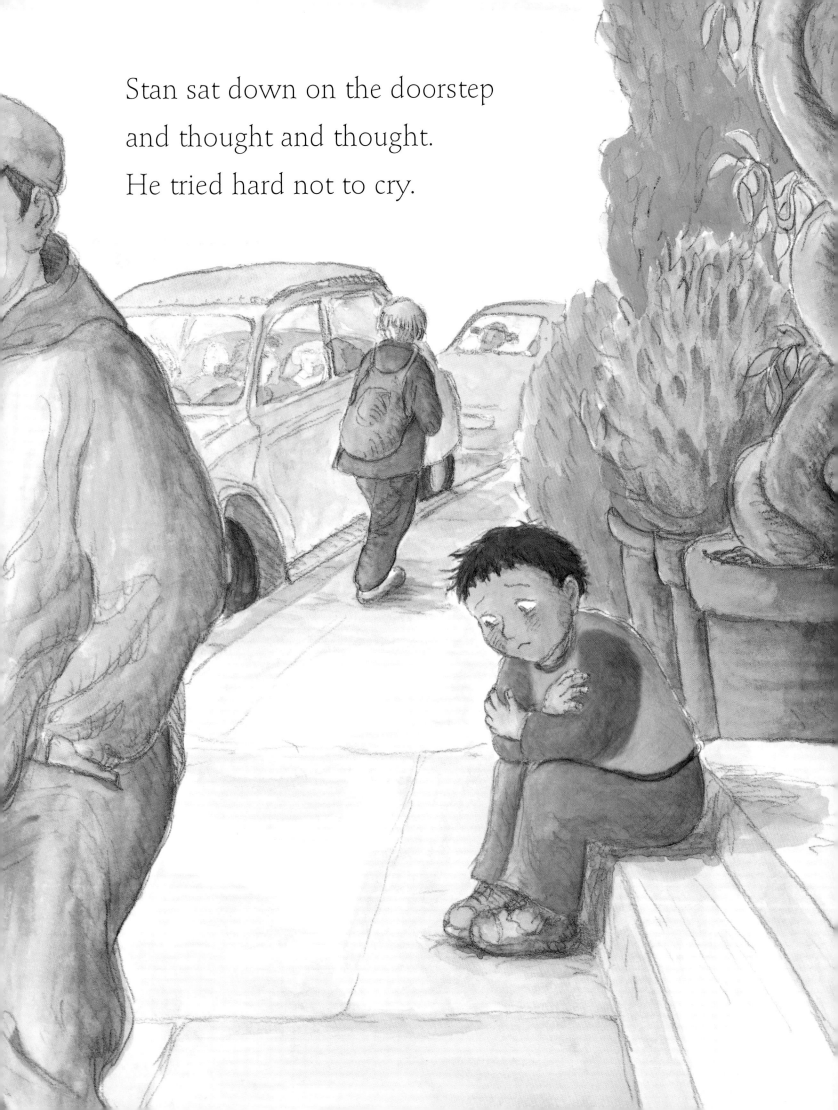

And then he heard a little noise.
It sounded like this, "Gooby-goo."

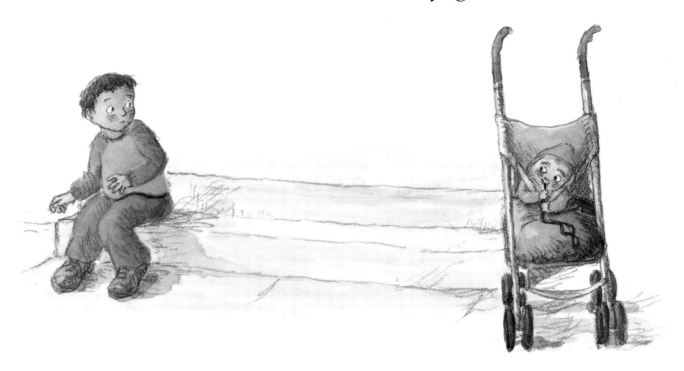

"What's up, Annie?" said Stan.
"Ooooo," said Annie.

"Annie?" said Stan.

"GLUB!" said Annie.

"Oh, ANNIE!" shouted Stan . . .

. . . and quick as a flash, he snatched the key.

"I've got it!" cried Stan.
"Don't worry, Gran!"
And he reached up high
and turned the key and
opened the door.
"Fantastic, Stan!" cried Gran.

Stan stood in the doorway. He heard the clock ticking.
He heard the cat purring. He saw his own special chair.
He saw the edge of his toy box beside the sofa.

He smelt the smell of Gran's house which was flowers
and old books and something nice cooking.
He was glad to be in Gran's house at last.

"How about a quiet game of cards now?" sighed Gran.
"Okay," said Stan. So they played Snap!

"Are you ready to play football?" asked Stan.
"Okay," said Gran.
Stan scored five goals and
Gran scored four.

At lunchtime, Gran made pancakes –
Stan's favourite meal.

After lunch, Gran did some work, Stan drew
a picture, and baby Annie
had a good kick with
her nappy off.

They had just finished reading a story
when BANG went the front door.
"Here I am! Sorry I'm late!"
called Mum.

"Hey, Mum!" said Stan. "Guess what? Gran lost the key and we couldn't get in and suddenly I saw Annie had it, but she nearly swallowed it, then I got it just in time . . .

. . . and I opened the door all by myself!"

"Oh, my poor baby!" cried Mum.

"Oh, my brave boy!"

"You are brave, Stan," said Gran, "and I'm giving you a key of your own now, so you can always open my front door whenever you want to."

"Thanks, Gran," said Stan.

"Boo-hoo!" sobbed baby Annie, because she didn't like being put in her car seat.

"See you soon, Stan," said Gran, as she kissed him goodbye.
"See you soon, Gran," said Stan.

That night, as the moon rose over the city and Mum rocked baby Annie to sleep, Stan told Dad the story of the lost key.

"Stan, you're quite a hero," said Dad,

as he carried him
up to bed.

Stan hid his key under his pillow.

He felt sleepy and happy.

"I think I'll go to Gran's house again soon," he said.

"Good idea," said Mum.

"Sweet dreams, Stan."